# Snuggle Piggy
## ☆ and ☆
# The Magic Blanket

by Michele Stepto

illustrated by John Himmelman

E. P. DUTTON · NEW YORK

for Rafael
M.S.

to my goddaughter, Danielle
J.H.

*Library of Congress Cataloging in Publication Data*
Stepto, Michele.
  Snuggle Piggy and the magic blanket.
  Summary: The creatures sewn onto Snuggle Piggy's magic
blanket, who come alive at night and dance with him in the
moonlight, are endangered one stormy night when the
blanket is left outdoors after being washed.
  [1. Blankets—Fiction.   2. Night—Fiction.   3. Pigs—
Fiction]   1. Himmelman, John, ill.   II. Title.
PZ7.S83667Sn   1987   [E]   86-23943
ISBN 0-525-44308-8

Published in the United States by E. P. Dutton,
2 Park Avenue, New York, N.Y. 10016

Published simultaneously in Canada by
Fitzhenry & Whiteside Limited, Toronto

Editor: Lucia Monfried     Designer: Isabel Warren-Lynch

Printed in Hong Kong by South China Printing Co.
First Edition     COBE     10 9 8 7 6 5 4 3 2 1

Once there was a little fellow named
Snuggle Piggy.

He lived with his Aunt Daisy in a bright blue
cottage near the edge of a quiet stream.

When Snuggle Piggy was very young—practically
brand-new!—Aunt Daisy made him a blanket out of
odds and ends to keep him warm at night. It was a
beautiful blanket, full of all the creatures in the
universe.

It had a bright moon floating in a clear blue sky, and stars, and an ocean, and a funny boat like a house.

In the center it had a man and a woman holding hands. The woman had red shoes and silvery earrings. The man had a long beard that looked terrifically bristly.

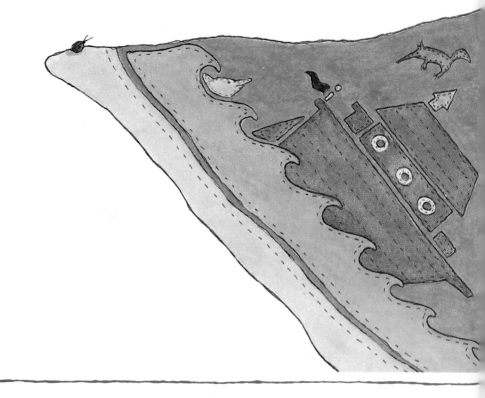

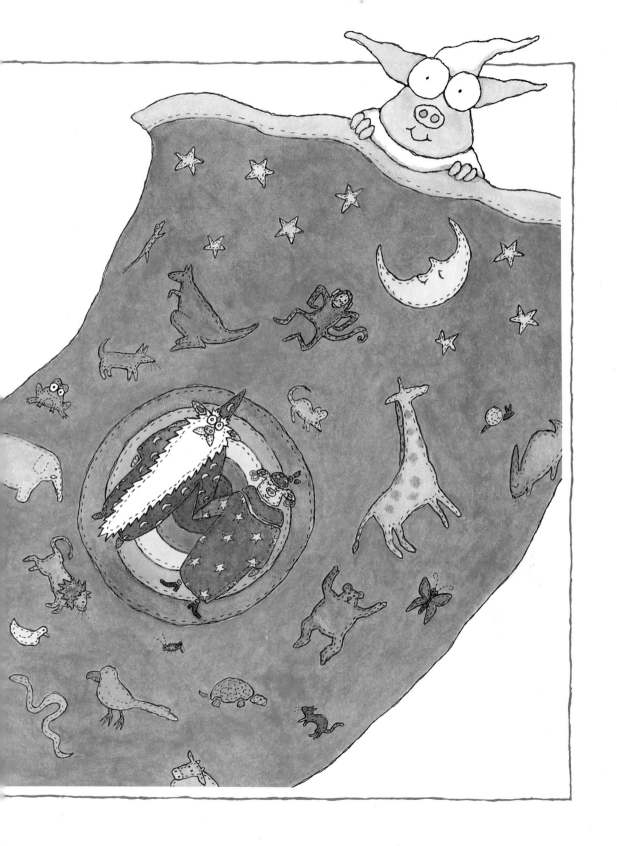

Every night, when Snuggle Piggy went to bed, Aunt Daisy tucked the blanket around him so that no cold drafts would get under the covers. Every morning, when he woke up, she folded the blanket inside out and hung it over the foot of the bed.

And once a week Aunt Daisy took the blanket down to the quiet stream and rubbed it and scrubbed it fresh and clean and hung it out to dry. Aunt Daisy took very good care of that blanket. She knew how much Snuggle Piggy liked it.

What Aunt Daisy didn't know was that it was a magic blanket. Every night, after she tucked Snuggle Piggy in bed and turned out the light, the man and the woman and all the creatures on the blanket came out to play with him.

They laughed and sang and danced in the clear moonlight. Each creature sang its own special song and danced its very own dance.

They taught Snuggle Piggy to dance too. And every night, he danced and danced until he danced himself to sleep. Snuggle Piggy loved his magic blanket. He never went to bed without it.

But one washing day, when Aunt Daisy had taken the blanket down to the stream and rubbed it and scrubbed it fresh and clean and hung it out to dry, it began to rain. It rained and it rained and it didn't stop raining, and that night Snuggle Piggy had to go to bed without his magic blanket.

"Don't worry, my Snuggle Piggy," said Aunt Daisy when she tucked him in bed. Then she gave him a big hug and kiss and turned out the light.

In the dark the rain came down even harder. Snuggle Piggy thought he could hear his friends calling for help.

He thought and he thought, and after a while he tiptoed out to the front door and opened it. *Crack! Crackle!* went the lightning. Snuggle Piggy could see the magic blanket flapping miserably in the wind and rain.

And quick as could be, he shot down the path to the stream. "I'm coming," he shouted. The thunder shouted back. The wind lashed the rain in angry circles around his head, but he grabbed the magic blanket in his arms and dashed back to the bright blue cottage.

Inside, Snuggle Piggy hung the blanket by the fire to dry. Its stars and moon were dark. The little boat still rocked crazily on its stormy sea. But not a single creature was missing.

Soon the blanket began to dry. His friends shook out their tails and scales and feathers and fur, and stretched out their hooves and their paws. The man patted his bristly beard dry in the warm glow. The woman took off her red shoes and wiggled her toes.

One by one Snuggle Piggy's friends fell asleep. At last he whispered "Good night, everyone" and tip-toed back to his bed.

Snuggle Piggy slept for hours and hours. When
he woke up, Aunt Daisy was folding his magic
blanket inside out over the foot of the bed. "Well,
my sleepyhead, good morning to you!" she said.

While Aunt Daisy made his breakfast porridge, Snuggle Piggy peeked inside the magic blanket, and what do you think he saw?

Everyone was there, safe and warm, the man and the woman and all the other creatures.

And above them in the sky was a bright yellow sun, dancing and shining, and next to it a beautiful rainbow.